Home for All Seasons

by Debbie Toews

FROM THE AUTHOR

Happy Spring! This is probably my favorite time of year, especially now, since we've moved up North! (I'm learning to appreciate warm weather more).

It's been a very busy the last 6 months, I can't wait to share my exciting news!

It started with our move from Oklahoma to Michigan (where my husband is originally from). We are now all settled in, complete with a wonderful old farmhouse and great view of all those neat old red barns! I know some of you have had trouble contacting me because of the change of address, (sorry for the inconvenience), so I will include all the new info at the bottom.

The last few months have been "really" busy...between finishing up Volume 8 and my "new" project, there has hardly been time to turn around!

I decided to take the plunge and open my own shop....and although it has made life a bit hectic, its also been a lot of fun getting things organized.

We found this wonderful old turn of the century building in downtown Alma (Michigan)....perfect with its old brick walls and beamed ceilings! And with the help of my talented brother-in-law (Thanks Tracy!) we turned the inside into something of an old barn!! The name **"Cobblestones"**... (what else, so fitting, since I love to paint them, don't you think)? I also have to pass on a big "Thank You" to my sister-in-laws and Mom-in-law for stocking the store while I worked on the book!

"Cobblestones" will have a full line of tole supplies, great country gifts (some hand painted!) and.....classes of course! So if your close, please stop by, have a cup of tea with us, take a class, watch a demonstration.....or just come by to say "Hi", we would love to meet you!

Hope to see you soon!

Deb

Contact Debbie at:
"Cobblestones"
325 N. State Street
Alma, Michigan 48801
(517) 466-9282 or debbie@CMSInter.net

For a list of my other books and seminar schedule, go to Eas'l's website at: **www.easlpublications.com**

Would you like to meet people who share the same love of painting as you?
Become a member of The Society of Decorative Painters. For more information write:
The Society of Decorative Painters
393 N. McLean Blvd. • Wichita, • KS 67203-5968

Distributed by: **Eas'l** ®
Essential Authors Services Ltd.
P.O. Box 22088 • St. Louis, MO • 63126
Phone: (314) 892-9222 • Fax: (314)892-9607
Visit our web site at: http:\\www.easlpublications.com

Project Index

Thermometer
Votive Pillar
from: **The Woodcrafter**
1522 Burlington-Jacksonville Rd.
Burlington, NJ 08016
(609) 387-9265

Sap Buckets and Blue Canning Jars
(Retail Only)
from: **Cobblestones**
325 N. State
Alma, MI 48801
(517) 466-9282

Crockery Lotion Dispenser
Crockery Birdhouse
Crockery Votive Cup
from: **Yesteryear's Pottery**
511 N. Washington
Marshall, TX 75671
(903) 935-7772

Oval Tin Planter
Rectangle Tin Tray
Gazebo
from: **Artists Club**
P.O Box 8930
Vancouver, WA 98668-8930
1 (800) 845-6507

Clay Pot
Concrete Stepping Stone
Concrete Edging
from: **Loew's Home Improvement
Centers**
(or any Home and Garden Center)

Cookie Tin
from: **Barb Watson**
20600 Avedida Hacinda
Riverside, CA 92508
e-mail: barb464@aol.com

Frame with pegs #200-0046
Picture Frame #24-3588
from: **Viking Woodcrafts**
1317 8th St. S.E.
Waseca, MN 56093
1-800-328-0016

Brushes
Loew-Cornell

- **Series 7350** Liner- 18/0 & 0
- **Series 7200** Fan- #2
- **Series 7300** Shaders- #'s 1, 2, 4, 6, 8, 10, 12
- **Series 7850** Stippler 1/8 OR an old worn flat brush

Other Painting Tools

2" foam pillow Form
(found at your local sewing or craft shop)
Old Toothbrush (or spatter tool) for snow

Basic Supplies

DecoArt Americana Acrylic,
  Metal, and Patio Paints
Krylon Spray Paint
DecoArt Duraclear Interior/Exterior Varnish
DecoArt Spray Sealer/ Finisher (gloss or matte,
your preference)
DecoArt Wood Sealer
Enviro-Tex Liquid Glass Finish (opt.)
Tracing Paper
Stylus
Transfer Paper (black & white)
Palette Paper
Masking Tape
Water Container and Paper Towels

General Painting Instructions

SKY

The skies are put in with spray paint. I do prefer the satin colors if I can get them .

It's fast, easy and makes a great base to paint on when working with slick surfaces!

I recommend Krylon Spray Paints if you can get them. And the instructions in the book will list the colors for Krylon, however, Krylon is not available in some places (like Canada!) so there are alternatives. "Floralife" (which is actually a floral spray works nicely too). For your convenience I have included the company address at the end of these instructions and also a retail source where it is available in Canada.

They have colors that are identical to the ones used in the book. Don't be afraid to experiment with different spray paints and colors, there are many on the market that will work very well, and you may find some new colors that will make beautiful sky colors!

When spraying in my sky, I use at least two different colors, and sometimes three. Your sky should have a graduation of color from darker at the top to a lighter shade as you get to the horizon.

Holding the can about 8 inches from the surface, start by spraying the darkest (blue) color in a small circular motion toward the top half of your painting surface, letting the colors dry thoroughly in between.

Spray in your second (or lighter) color toward the bottom half of the blue. Leave about an inch or two of blue showing at the top. A third shade may be used if you wish, spray this in the middle of the second shade, again, leaving about and inch of the second shade showing at the top (of the third).

The "trick" to this is to be able to get your colors up far enough on the painting surface, so when you put your tree line in, you will see all of the colors in between the trees! You don't have to see a lot of the second or third color. Just so it "peeks" in between the trees some where!

It will be best if you will spray two light coats of each color, rather than one heavy one, that way you will avoid any drips. However, if drips should occur, just smooth them out with your finger, usually the trees and grass cover any little mistakes. Practice on a piece of cardboard or an old jar before spraying onto the project.

Floralife Inc.
751 Thunderbolt Drive.
Walterboro, SC 29489366
1 (800) 323-3689

Krafty Kennedys
(Floralife retailer)
2711 Dingman Dr.
London, ON Canada N6N 1G3
1 (519) 681-0015 or
kraftyk@akcad.on.ca

PATTERN PLACEMENT

Trace pattern from the book using your tracing paper and a pencil. Center tracing on your painting surface, being careful not to cover all the colors in your sky. Trace on the trees and horizon line first with the transfer paper using a stylus. These will be painted in before tracing on the rest of the pattern.

Trace on the structures, paths, fences, etc, (over the painted trees) with white transfer paper (use black if doing a snow scene.)

TREES

All trees (with the exception of the pines)
are put in with a sponge.

I prefer using a two inch foam pillow form to sponge with, which can be bought at any sewing center. The texture of a pillow form is perfect.

Tear off a piece from the pillow form about two-inches in width and roll it up to form a loose ball. Pick up paint, (base color, the darkest for depth), and pat in tree line working from horizon up. Be careful not to make trees too uniform, vary the size and shapes.

Either pick up a new piece of sponge, (or pat out all of the base color on a paper towel), before picking up the next color. Load highlight color on the top half of the sponge. If you are working with a "double load" (summer trees), dip sponge in the green first, yellow second, tipping the sponge up when dipping in yellow so that it loads on the very tip. Pat a couple of times on the palette before sponging directly on the painting surface. This helps you to see what you are getting. Pat in "arcs" of color toward tops of trees working down. If it blends together too much pick up more highlight color and repeat the process. Careful not to overdo the highlight colors! You don't want to lose the darkness in the background or you will lose your depth!

PINE TREES

Pine trees are put in with the 10/0 liner and an old worn flat brush or a stippler. I use the liner to form the very top and first few small boughs. Pick up the worn brush and stipple in the rest of the tree. Again, be careful not to get these too uniform.

SHRUBBERY AND FLOWERS

These are stippled in with a worn #2 or #4 shader brush. If you don't have a worn brush, a small (1/8) stippler from Loew-Cornell works well. "Stipple" by picking up color and "pouncing" on a heavy coat of paint, varying the size and shape of the foliage.

For flowers wash out brush and double load. Pick up the bright color first, then tip in white. Pat a couple of times on the palette to blend a little, but you still want to maintain the white (or highlight) color on tops of slopes.

BASECOATING

With a flat brush pick up the color and brush on one or two smooth, even coats of paint. Keep strokes going with the contour of the structure. All buildings should show a good contrast between the "light" side and the "shaded" side. The size of brush will depend on the size of structure you are painting. Use whatever brush size you are most comfortable with, but keep in mind, the larger the brush, the faster you will cover the area.

STREAKING

This is done to give the building a "weathered" or "board" look. Using your flat brush, pick up a very small amount of paint, and gently "streak" on the color in a "hit and miss" fashion. A rake brush also works great for this if you have one!

SHADING

Shading is used under a roof line (eaves) to give the illusion of a shadow. Use a small flat brush and pick up a very thin wash of black paint. Put a stroke or two on your palette to pull most of the paint out of the brush. Very gently pull this down under the eave, roof line or any place you need to cast a shadow. It works a lot like a float, only you are loading the whole brush with very transparent black. The width of the brush you use will be the width of the shadow, so chose accordingly.

DETAIL LINEWORK

All detail work, framing windows, outlining, windmills, etc., are done with a 10/0 liner brush.

When doing any linework, thin your paint enough that it will flow like ink. If you roll the tip of the brush in paint it will make a finer line. The longer and faster you can make your line the straighter it will become! Most window and door frames will be outlined (or underlined) with a dark line of paint. This defines the frame more and gives it an outer edge! It will make your painting a little more three dimensional!

PATHS

Scrub in paths starting at the top and working down using the edge of a flat brush. Keep the brush moving form left to right. Strokes should be "choppy" and uneven to give the appearance of dirt. Edges of the path should be darker than middle of path. To make it recede to the background, make it larger at the bottom as it comes toward you. It also helps if you curve it just a bit. If you work the paint too much it will blend together more than it should and make the path too "smooth" looking.

USING THE FAN BRUSH

FOR GRASS

Lay in the grass with the indicated color using a fan brush. Dampen your brush just a little, pick up color and "pat" in starting at the top, working down. Wipe out brush and pick up highlight color. Pat this in toward the "tops" of the slopes, blending down. Work in a "typewriter" motion form left to right and down. Pat until the colors blend together nicely, you do not want to see a definite line where one color stops and the

other starts! I wash out my brush when going from a dark to a light color, otherwise I just wipe out the paint on a paper towel. Keep in mind that shaded areas will be on the shaded side of the structures and the underside of slopes!

SNOW

I always start by brushing on a couple of basecoats of white (letting them dry thoroughly in between coats) before laying in the snow. This is especially helpful if you are working on a slick surface. Start by laying in the white with a large flat brush. Brush in the shaded area with color indicated and blend softly together. Add more "highlight" (white) on tops of slopes with corner of brush. Moisten your brush or thin the paint just a bit to make the blending easier. Too much moisture will cause the paint to "lift" from the surface though! Its helpful if you work one small area at a time.

FINISHES
CROCKERY

The crockery in this book is finished with Aristocrat High Gloss Finish (see supply list). It is a liquid (not a spray) that is packaged in a box including two bottles, a resin and a hardener that you will mix together in equal parts. The kit may be found at your local hobby store or home improvement center.

Lay the crock, painting side face up, and pour some of the mixture on (about the size of a quarter). With an old brush (or small piece of cardboard) spread it over the painted area only. It will have many tiny bubbles on the surface. To break these either blow on the finish through a straw or hold a small house-hold propane torch a few inches from the painting and move it back and forth briefly over the surface. (Small "throw-away" torches are widely available in the hardware sections of your local store and are relatively inexpensive.) They are simple and safe to use! It will take only a few seconds and you will see the bubbles breaking. This will give you a beautiful clear finish! Leave it setting like this for 24 hours until it completely hard-ens.

For the first 30 minutes or so, until it tacks up, you may want to check your piece and wipe any drips that may occur down the side. This is a little more trouble than a conventional spray finish but is much more durable and completely washable. You will find that it will intensify the colors and give a beautiful, shiny, glasslike appearance. There are also very thorough directions included in each box.

WOOD AND METAL PIECES

Most all of the wood and metal pieces in the book have been finished with DecoArt Acrylic Spray Sealer/Finisher. It comes in either gloss or matte finish. Some of the pieces that would be painted for outside decoration were finished with DecoArt DuraClear Interior/Exterior Varnish.

Long Awaited Spring
tray
color photo on front cover • pattern on following pages

Paint Palette

Krylon Spray Paints
#3505 Colonial Blue Satin   #3506 Rose Satin
#1509 Navajo White

DecoArt Americana

French Grey Blue	Jade Green
Titanium White	Petal Pink
Limeade	Midnight Green
Honey Brown	Bittersweet Chocolate
Uniform blue	Lamp Black
Deep Periwinkle	Royal Fuchsia
Yellow Light	

Special Supplies

Metal Tray
2" Foam Pillow Form (for sponging trees)
DecoArt Spray Sealer/Finisher

Preparation

No preparation necessary, tray is already primed.

Painting Instructions

SKY
Spray in sky starting at the top working across and down a few inches with Colonial Blue. When blue is dry, spray in Rose Satin, leaving at least 2 inches of blue showing at the top. Next spray in the Navajo White extending this a little more than half way down the tray.

TREES
Trees are patted in with a small piece of sponge using Jade Green + touch of French Blue Grey. Start at the horizon and work up varying the size and shapes.
Highlight with Jade tipped in White and Petal Pink + White, using a new piece of sponge for each color change.

BACKGROUND MEADOW
Using a #2 mini fan pat in grass with Jade Green + Limeade. As you work toward the bottom of the hill pick up a bit of Midnight Green on the brush and pat this in for shading. Wash out brush and highlight top of hill by patting in Limeade + touch of White, patting down, until it blends into the base color.

COTTAGE
Cottage is based in using the #6 and White + touch of Honey Brown on the left.
Right (or shaded) sides are White +touch of Honey + touch of Bittersweet Chocolate. Mix your paint loosely so it looks a bit "streaky" for texture!

Roof is painted in with Uniform Blue, shading by pulling up from the bottom with Uniform Blue + touch of Black. Highlight top of roof by pulling from top edge, down, with White, blending into the blue.

Window and underneath eave is brushed in with the #2 and Black + touch of White. Crossbars in the window are inky White, painted using the 18/0 liner.

Also with the liner frame the roof and window with Uniform Blue + White and paint on trim with Uniform Blue. Cast a shadow under the roof with the #4 and a thin wash of Black.

Chimney is based in with the #4 and Lamp Black. Stones are formed using the same brush loading with Honey Brown tipped in White. Form rocks loosely varying the shapes and keeping the highlight (White) toward the top of the rock.

Cast a shadow (with the #4) down the right side of the chimney with a wash of Black.

WATER
Paint in water using a #10 and an equal mix of French Grey

Blue + White, brushing from right to left. Darken edges of water by pulling in from the outer edge, blending into the water, with French Grey Blue + touch of Black.

Wash out the brush and highlight the middle by streaking across lightly with White.

This will give the water the appearance of "ripples". Paint in shore line by scrubbing in Raw Sienna + touch of Bittersweet Chocolate. (You may want to wait and paint in shore line after you have you have brushed in the rest of the grass. This will help to "set it in").

FOREGROUND GRASS

Foreground grass is painted in the same manner as the meadow in the background. Use the same shades, casting shadows with the Midnight Green under the slopes and to the right side of the cottage.

BRIDGE

Use the #6 to base in bridge with Black. Stones are laid in with the #4 loading the brush with Honey Brown tipping the top edge of brush in White. Lay them in like a jigsaw puzzle varying the shapes. Outline the top left of the bridge with a thin line of Grey (White + touch of Black) to show the top edge. Make sure you see a little of the Black edge showing on the right sides under the bridge for a more three dimensional look.

FLOWERS

Stipple in foliage for flowers using an old worn brush and Jade + a touch of Midnight Green. Highlight foliage with Jade. Flowers are stippled on using alternate shades of Yellow Light tipped in White, Royal Fuchsia tipped in White, and Deep Periwinkle tipped in White. Wildflowers in the grass are pounced on with the very tip of the fan brush using Deep Periwinkle tipped in White.

RAINBOW

Paint in rainbow using the #4 and thin washes of French Grey Blue + White, Yellow Light +White, and Petal Pink + White. Try to form each color in one long brush stroke reaching from one group of trees to the other so you won't see where it stops and starts.

FINISHING

Pull a few branches in the trees with the 18/0 liner and thinned Bittersweet Chocolate.
Birds are formed with the liner and Black.
Spray with a coat of DecoArt Finisher/Sealer.

© Debbie Toews

Simple Elegance
basket
color photo on front cover • pattern on following pages

Paint Palette

Krylon Spray Paints

#3505 Colonial Blue Satin   #3506 Rose Satin
#1509 Navajo White

DecoArt Americana

Jade Green	Yellow Light
Titanium White	Baby Pink
Country Blue	Deep Periwinkle
Slate Grey	Lamp black
Raw Sienna	Buttermilk
Avocado	Hauser Dark Green
Bittersweet Chocolate	True Blue
Royal Fuchsia	Lavender
Dioxazine Purple	Light French Blue
French Mauve	

Special Supplies

2" foam pillow form (for sponging trees)
Wire Basket with Wood Lid
DecoArt Spray Sealer/Finisher

Preparation

Sand any rough edges on wooden lid. Base coat lid with Light French Blue.

Painting Instructions

SKY

Spray in sky starting at top with Colonial Blue. Next spray in Rose Satin, leaving at least 2 inches of blue showing at the top. Last, spray in Navajo White, extending this about 3/4 way down the lid.

BACKGROUND TREES

Using a small piece of sponge, rolled to form a loose ball, start at the bottom and work up, sponging in trees with Jade Green + touch of Light French Blue. Vary the sizes and shapes of the trees.

Highlight, using a new piece of sponge. With Jade Green tipped in a touch of White, and Baby Pink tipped in White, form "arches" of color starting at the top of the tree and working down. Not too heavy though, this is where the sun "catches" on the tree and forms a "highlight"!

HOUSE

Base in house using a #10 flat and Country Blue. Wash out brush, picking up just a touch of White and streaking down the house lightly for added texture.

Roof is Titanium White, pulling up from the bottom with Slate Grey, (blending back into the White), for shading.

Door is brushed in with the #4 and Titanium White. Paint in windows and chimney with the #4 and Lamp Black. Curtains in downstairs windows are brushed in with the #2 and a transparent wash of White.

Shutters and window box are French Mauve, streaking the shutters (horizontally) with a touch of White for texture.

Frame windows and paint in crossbars with inky White using the 18/0 liner.

Frame and trim roof and door with Deep Periwinkle and French Mauve.

Underline or outline all framing with a thin line of inky Black for more definition.

Paint in porch and steps with Slate Grey.

Cast shadows under roof, on the door, and to the right side of windows with the #4 and a transparent wash of Black.

Paint in gingerbread trim at the top and porch railings with thinned White and the 18/0 liner.

Stones on the chimney are formed with the the #2 loading with Raw Sienna tipping in Buttermilk. Lay them in loosely, keeping the Buttermilk to the top of the stone. Outline top of Chimney with the liner and Raw Sienna + Buttermilk.

FOREGROUND TREES

Use an old brush or small stipple brush to form trees. Stipple in with Avocado, shading to the right by stippling on Hauser Dark Green + touch of Black. Blend the shading into the Avocado. Wash out brush pick up Yellow Light + White, laying

this in on the left and stippling over, blending into the base color again.

Tree trunks are formed with the liner using Bittersweet Chocolate on the right and highlighting on the left with Raw Sienna + Buttermilk.

PATH

Base coat path with the #10 using Black + touch of Bittersweet Chocolate.

Flagstones are formed with the #4, loading brush in Raw Sienna, tipping in Buttermilk. Keep the "light" towards the top of the stone. Stones closest to the house are smaller, thin and flat in shape. Make them a little larger as you work down, but careful not to paint them too round, you will lose your depth!

GRASS

Use a #2 fan brush to pat in grass. Load with Avocado, pouncing from right to left and down. As you work down, pick up

Hauser Dark Green + Black. Wipe out brush pat gently where the two colors meet to blend.

Highlight along the edge of path and along horizon with Yellow Light. Again, pat gently to blend into the base color.

FLOWERS

Stipple in foliage for flowers using an old brush and Hauser Dark Green + touch of Black. Highlight with Yellow Light. Wash out brush, stipple on flowers using alternate colors of Royal Fuchsia tipped in White, Lavender + Dioxazine Purple tipped in White, and True Blue tipped in White.

FINISHING

Pull a few tree branches through the trees with inky Bittersweet Chocolate using the liner brush.

Spray with DecoArt Spray Sealer/Finisher.

© Debbie Toews

Birdhouse Collector
wooden frame
color photo on inside front cover • pattern on next page

Paint Palette

DecoArt Americana

Buttermilk	Lamp Black
Arbor Green	Titanium White
French Mauve	French Grey Blue
Midnight Blue	Dark Chocolate
Moon Yellow	Raw Sienna
Burgundy Wine	

Special Supplies

Wood frame
DecoArt Weathered Wood Crackle Medium
DecoArt Spray Sealer/Finisher

Preparation:

Sand any rough edges.

Painting Instructions

FRAME

Using a large brash, basecoat entire frame with Lamp Black. When dry, add a heavy coat of DecoArt Weathered Wood Crackle. Allow to dry to touch (45 minutes to 1 hour). Apply topcoat of Buttermilk with the large brush, being careful not to work over any area where you have already applied color (Buttermilk). Load brush heavy enough that you can apply paint in one long brushstroke! Let dry thoroughly before putting pattern on.

GREEN BIRDHOUSE

With a #10 base in right side of house Arbor Green. Streak lightly with Buttermilk for added texture. Base in left side with Arbor + touch of Black.
Paint roof Titanium White, shading at bottom by pulling up from edge with White + touch of Black.
Use an 0 liner to paint in bird hole with Black. Frame roof edge, bird hole and paint on trim with thinned White using the liner brush.
Underline framing with a thin line of Black for added definition.
Cast a shadow under roof with the #6 and a transparent wash of Black.

PINK BIRDHOUSE

Basecoat house with the # 10 and French Mauve. With a #4 and a wash of White lay in bricks. Shade bottom of bricks with a float of Burgundy Wine.
Paint in roof with Dark Chocolate. Highlight top edge of roof with a float of White. Brush in bird hole with the #4 and Lamp Black.
Using the #6 "cast a shadow" under the roof line with a wash of Black using the width of the brush.

With thinned White and the 18/0 liner paint on trim and frame bird hole.
Outline bird hole on left with a thin line of Black to bring it forward.

BLUE BIRDHOUSE

Base in birdhouse with French Grey Blue. Paint in stripes with Midnight Blue. Frame roof with the #2 and White. Paint in bird hole with Black.

Using the 18/0 frame bird hole, paint a thin line of White down the left side of each dark stripe and paint in a horizontal line of White across birdhouse.

Outline, under roof, and to the left of the White lines with a thin line of Black for more definition.
Using the #6 and a thin wash of Black, "cast a shadow" under the roof and also under the horizontal white stripe.

Vines and leaves are painted with Arbor Green using the 18/0 liner. Highlight leaves with a float of White. Paint rosebuds with the #2 and French Mauve. Inside of bud (top) is Burgundy Wine. Outline top and down the middle for a "petal" effect with the liner brush and White.

Cast a shadow under roof with the #6 and a thin wash of Black.

WATERING CAN

Base watering can with the #8 shader and 0 liner using Moon Yellow.
Shade down right and left sides with a wash of Dark Chocolate. Highlight middle of can, top of spout and top of can with the #4 and a float of White. Paint inside of can a dark Grey (White + Black). Shade inside of handle and bottom of spout with Dark Chocolate. Outline edge of opening with a thin line of White using the 18/0 liner.

ROSES

Paint in roses with the #6 and French Mauve. Float "commas" of White, starting in the middle, working around to the outside edge. Float in shading under the petal with Burgundy Wine.
Paint in leaves with Arbor Green, shading with Arbor + touch of Black. Highlight with Arbor + White. Veins in leaves are thinned Arbor + Black using the 18/0 liner.
Vines and stems are Arbor + Black.

FINISHING

Spray with DecoArt Spray Sealer/Finisher.

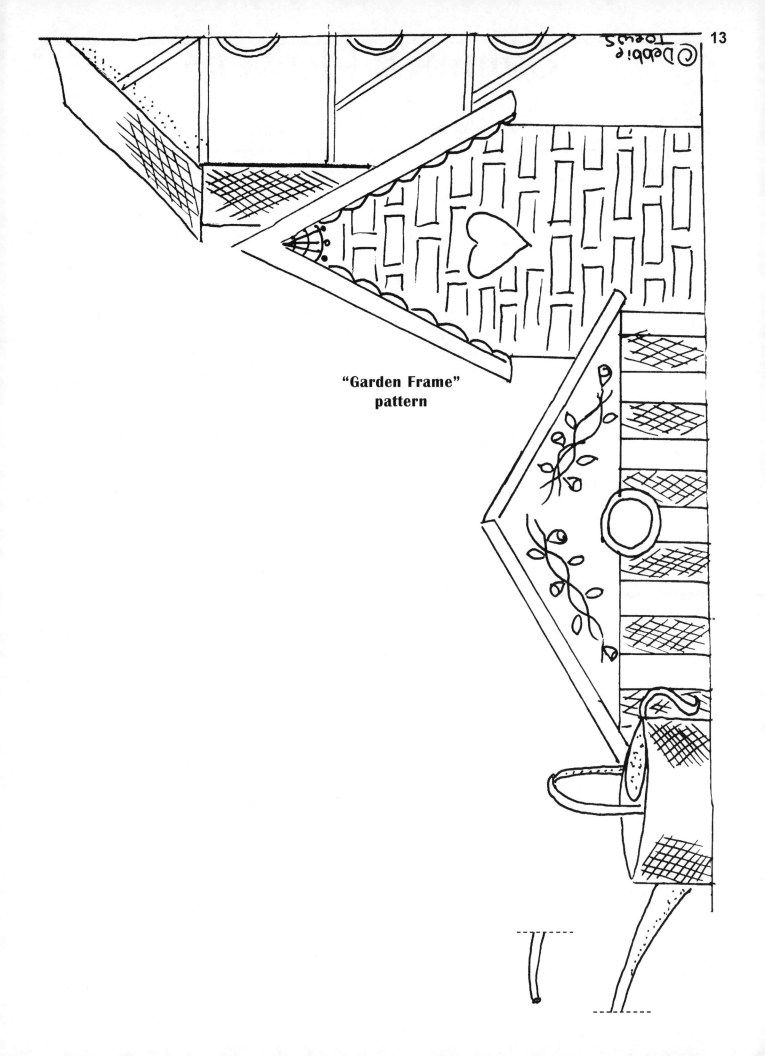

© Debbie Toews

"Garden Frame"
pattern

Summer Flowers
votive pillar
color photo on inside front cover • pattern on this page

Paint Palette
Krylon Spray Paints
#3505 Colonial Blue Satin
#3506 Rose Satin

DecoArt Americana
Yellow Light
Midnight Green
Limeade
Jade Green
Heritage Brick
Bittersweet Chocolate
Titanium White
Lamp Black
Royal Fuchsia
Dioxazine Purple
Lavender
Brilliant Red
True Blue

Special Supplies
Wood Votive Pillar
DecoArt Spray Sealer/Finisher
DecoArt Wood Sealer

Preparation
Sand any rough edges with fine sandpaper. Seal with DecoArt wood sealer.

Painting Instructions
SKY
Spray in sky with Colonial Blue Satin extending this about 1/4 way down from the top of the pillar. Next, spray in Rose Satin. Let dry thoroughly.

TREES
Sponge in depth of trees using Bittersweet Chocolate + touch of Midnight Green.
Highlight with a new piece of sponge and Jade Green, starting at the top, forming arches of color, but leaving enough darkness in between highlights for depth.
Add extra highlight on top of the Jade with Limeade tipped in Yellow Light. Pat this off on the palette before patting onto surface so the coat of paint isn't too heavy.

HOUSE
Base in left side of house with the #10 and White. Right side is White + touch of Black. Streak left side of house lightly with

the dark mix for added texture.
Windows, door and underneath eaves are painted in with the #4 and Black.
Roof is brushed in with Heritage Brick, shading at the bottom by pulling up with Heritage Brick + touch of Black. Highlight top with Heritage + White pulling down from top edge blending into the base color.
Frame roof, windows, and door with Heritage + White. Underline to the right and bottom of window frames and under right side of roof frame with a thin line of Black for added definition. Add a thin line of White down the inside of the door and window frames for an edge. Crossbars in window are also White.
Cast a shadow under roof with the #6 and a transparent wash of Black.

GRASS
Pat in grass with the #2 mini fan and Jade Green. As you work down pick up Midnight Green for shading, patting and blending this back up into the Jade.
Wash out brush, pick up Limeade + Yellow Light and pat across the top (horizon) blending down into the Jade for added highlight.

FLOWERS
Stipple in foliage using an old worn brush and Midnight Green + touch of Bittersweet Chocolate. Highlight foliage with Jade Green + Yellow Light.
Wash out brush, stipple on flowers in varying shades of Dioxazine Purple + Lavender tipped in White, Royal Fuchsia tipped in White and Brilliant Red tipped in White. The delphiniums are stippled in with True Blue, making small petals over this with the liner and True Blue + White.

FENCE
Paint in fence with the liner brush and thinned White.

FINISHING
Pull a few branches in trees with the 18/0 liner and thinned Raw Sienna.
Birds are Lamp Black.
Finish by painting the top and bottom of pillar with the #12 and Jade Green + touch of White.
Spray with DecoArt Finisher/Sealer.

Butterfly Garden
sap bucket
color photo on inside front cover • pattern on following page

Paint Palette

DecoArt Metal Paints

Cornflower Blue	Bright Yellow
Coal Black	Bright Orange
Strawberry Shake	Sunlight Yellow
Fresh Lavender	Real Red
Deep Fuchsia	Bright Blue
Bright White	Hunter Green
Deep Blue	Sage Green
Expresso Bean	Ivory
Burnt Sienna	Clear Medium

Special Supplies

Metal Sap Bucket
2" foam pillow form (for sponging trees)

Preparation

Wash bucket in warm soapy water, rinsing thoroughly to remove any residue.

Painting Instructions

*Thin paints with the clear medium.

SKY

Sponge in sky using a large piece of sponge torn from the pillow foam.
Start at the top with Cornflower Blue working down about 4 inches. Pick up a new piece of sponge and Strawberry Shake patting this color in next. Last, pick up Sunlight Yellow (with a new piece of sponge) patting about 3/4 way down the bucket. Again, pick up a new sponge to pat each color together so they blend one
into the other.

TREES

Using a small piece of sponge rolled to form a loose ball, pat in background of trees with Hunter Green + a touch of Deep Blue. Let dry and sponge on another coat (this should be fairly heavy since it is the "depth" of the trees). Start at the bottom and work up, varying the size and shapes of the trees. Highlight (using a new piece of sponge) with Sage Green + Bright White.

FOREGROUND TREES

Stipple in trees using an old worn flat brush (a #6 or 8 will work best). Start on the right, or shaded, side with Hunter + touch of Deep Blue + touch of Black. As you stipple over toward the middle, wipe out brush and pick up Sage Green blending the two shades together. Use Sage + Sunlight Yellow to highlight down the left side for added "sunlight". Tree branches are made with the liner, starting on the right side with Expresso Bean, working over toward the left with Expresso + Ivory.

HOUSE

Base in the left side of house with the #10 using Bright White. The right side is White + touch of Black. Streak the left side lightly with the dark mix for added texture. Base in the roof using an equal mix of Expresso Bean + Bright Yellow.
Shade by pulling from the bottom up with Expresso + touch of Black. Highlight top of roof by pulling down with Ivory, blending one color into the other.

Door on the right is Expresso, brushed in with the #4 flat. Window in the door is White + touch of Black. Other windows are painted in with Black. Frame
windows and door using the base roof color (Expresso + Bright Yellow). Crossbars in window are Ivory. Chimney is based in on the left with Burnt Sienna + touch of Ivory. Shaded side is darkened with a touch of Black. Separate bricks with thin lines of Black using the 18/0 liner. "Cast a shadow" under roof using a #6 flat and a thin, transparent "wash" of Black.

SHRUBS

Stipple in foliage for shrubbery using the worn brush and Hunter + touch of Black. Highlight using Sage + Sunlight. Wash out brush, stipple on flowers with Fresh Lavender tipped in White.

GRASS

Paint in grass using the #10 and a mix of Hunter + touch of Black. Highlight on tops of slopes and toward horizon with Sage + Sunlight Yellow + touch of White.
Blend your highlight color softly down into the dark so its looks like an easy graduation of color. If your highlight blends into the base color too much, go back when it starts to tack up a bit and add more highlight, again, blending down.

BUTTERFLY HOUSE

Butterfly house is painted in the same manner as the house, only using smaller brushes (#4 & liner). Left side is White, right side, White + touch of Black.
Roof is the same color as the house, highlighting top by pulling down with Ivory.
Underneath eave and butterfly holes are painted in with the liner and Black.
Frame roof with the roof color + Ivory to lighten.
Post is painted with the #2 using Expresso + touch of Black on the right, using short choppy strokes so that it has the appearance of old wood. As you work over pick up Burnt Sienna + Ivory for the highlight color, chopping this down the left side, blending over into the dark.

BUTTERFLY

Paint in butterfly with the liner brush, and Bright Orange. Outline and paint details with Black.

FLOWERS

Stipple in foliage using the old brush or a small piece of sponge.

16

Background color is Hunter + touch of Black.
Highlight foliage with Hunter +Bright Yellow.
Flowers are stippled on using a variety of shades:
Real Red + Deep Fuchsia tipped in
White, Bright Yellow tipped in
White, Fresh Lavender +
Fuchsia tipped in White and
Bright Blue. ("Delphiniums"
are stippled in with the Bright
Blue using a liner and Bright
Blue + White to form
the petals).

FINISHING
Branches in the trees are formed with thinned
Expresso using the 18/0 liner. Birds are Black.
You can use the clear medium to "varnish" it
with if you want, but the metal paints are
quite durable and really don't require a
finishing coat.

© Debbie Toews

Spring Dispenser
crockery lotion dispenser
color photo on inside front cover • pattern on this page

Paint Palette

Krylon Spray Paints
#3505 Colonial Blue Satin
#3506 Rose Satin
#1808 Maize

DecoArt Americana

French Blue Grey	Jade Green
Titanium White	Petal Pink
Pineapple	Raw Sienna
Lamp Black	Uniform Blue
Midnight Green	Tree Blue
Royal Fuchsia	Deep Periwinkle
Brilliant Red	

Special Supplies

Crockery Dispenser
2" foam pillow form (for sponging in trees)
Duraclear Varnish or Enviro Tex Lite (for a glass like finish)

Preparation

No preparation necessary other than washing crockery to remove any residue.

Painting Instructions

SKY

Spray in sky starting with the Colonial Blue, using a small circular motion, staying at least 6-8 inches away from the surface of the crock. When dry spray in Rose Satin (toward the upper middle of the blue), next spray in Navajo White, letting these dry thoroughly before placing a pattern on.

TREES

Pat in trees in using a small piece of rolled sponge with French Blue Grey + Jade Green + touch of White. Highlight trees with "arches" of color using a new sponge for each color. Highlight shades will either be Jade Green + White or Petal Pink + White (double loading the sponge, with the White towards the top). Use a very light amount of paint for the highlights, pat your sponge off on the palette before sponging onto the surface to remove any excess paint.

HOUSE

Using a #6 shader, brush in left side of house with Pineapple. The right (or shaded) side is Pineapple + touch of Raw Sienna. Wash out brush and streak down lightly over the left side with a bit of White for added texture. With the #2 paint in windows and underneath eave with Black + touch of White. Paint in roof (using the #6 again) with Uniform Blue. Shade roof by pulling up from the bottom with Uniform Blue + touch of Black, blending into the base color. Highlight by pulling down with Uniform + touch of White, again blending from one shade to the next. Shutters are also painted in with Uniform Blue (#2) and streaked across with a bit of White for texture.

Using the 18/0 liner frame roof with a thin line of White + touch of Uniform Blue. Underline framing on right with a thin line of Black.

Frame right side of window and paint in crossbars with White. Outline right side of shutter edge with a thin line of Black for added definition.

Cast a shadow under the left side of roof with the #4 and a thin wash of Black.

FENCE & TRELLIS

Paint in fence and trellis with the 18/0 liner and thinned Titanium White.

FLOWERS

Using an old worn brush, stipple in foliage for flowers with Midnight Green. Highlight with Jade Green.

Flowers are stippled using the same brush and alternate colors of True Blue tipped in White, Deep Periwinkle tipped in White, Royal Fuchsia tipped in White and Brilliant Red tipped in White.

FINISHING

Pull a few branches in the trees with the liner and thinned Raw Sienna.

Birds arc Lamp Black.

Finish crockery with the Duraclear Interior Exterior Varnish, or if you prefer a glossier shine, the Enviro-Tex Lite.

© Debbie Toews

Frosty Morning

slate

color photo on page 21 • pattern on the following page

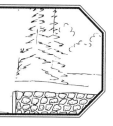

Paint Palette

Krylon Spray Paints
#3505 Colonial Blue Satin
#3501 Navy Satin

DecoArt Americana

Titanium White	Midnight Green
Brilliant Red	Lamp Black
French Grey Blue	Terra Cotta
Yellow Light	Bittersweet Chocolate
Oxblood	Khaki Tan

Special Supplies

Slate
2" foam pillow form (for sponging trees)
DecoArt Spray Sealer/Finisher

Painting Instructions

SKY

Spray top half of slate with Navy Satin. When dry, spray Colonial Blue toward the top middle, leaving at least 1 or 2 inches of Navy showing at the top.

BACKGROUND TREES

Pat in trees using the sponge and Khaki Tan + touch of White. Add extra White to tops of trees for "snow". Work from horizon, up, making trees lighter as you work up towards the top. Vary the sizes and shapes as you work across.

BACKGROUND PINES

Using a mix of French Grey Blue, Touch of Midnight Green + White, form the tops of the pines and first few boughs with the 18/0 liner.
Use an old brush to stipple in rest of pine, starting at the middle and working each bough out. Wash out brush, pick up a bit of White and stipple on "snow".
*Basecoat ground area with White.

COTTAGE

Use a #10 to base in right sides Slate Grey. Left side is Slate Grey + touch of Black. Windows are painted in with the #4 double loading with Yellow Light and Brilliant Red. (Keep the red on the left side since this is the shaded side).
Use a #2 to paint in the underneath eaves, Black.
Rocks are formed with the #4 loaded with Terra Cotta, tipped in White.
Rocks on the shaded side are Bittersweet Chocolate tipped in Terra Cotta.
Keep the light on the top of the rock, working several before you pick up paint again. As you work, if you loose your White, pick up a bit more and go back over the tops of the

rocks for added highlight.
Basecoat roof with the #8 and Titanium White. Pull shading (French Grey Blue),
from the bottom edge, up, blending into the White.
Chimney is Oxblood + touch of Buttermilk on the right and Oxblood + touch of Black on the left. Separate bricks with thin lines of Black using the 18/0 liner.
Also use the liner to "frame" the roof with White, underlining this framing with a thin line of Black for more definition.
There are small candles in the window painted with the liner and White, flames are Brilliant Red.
Frame the windows and paint in crossbars with thinned Black. Cast a shadow under roof line with the #6 and a thin wash of Black.

PINES & SHRUBBERY

Pines are painted in the same manner as the background pines only using Midnight Green and White for the snow. Shrubs are stippled in with an old worn brush, also stippling on a bit of White for snow. Berries are small dots of Brilliant Red.

PATH

Scrub in path with the #10 working from right to left with a mix of Bittersweet Chocolate, French Grey Blue, + White. This should be light and hazy in color.
Work on the edge of the brush, making the path turn a little and get larger as you work down.

SNOW

Lay in snow using a #12 with Titanium White. As you work down and under the pines and shrubs, pull in a bit of shading with French Grey Blue. Blend this down into the White, picking up a little moisture on the brush if needed for blending the colors.

ROCK FENCE

Base in fence area with the #12 and Slate Grey + touch of Black.
Rocks are formed in the same manner as the house, using the #8 brush loaded with Terra Cotta tipped in White. Again, you should be able to work a few stones before picking up more color, but you may loose your highlight. Tip your brush in a bit more White and go back over the tops of some of the rocks for added highlight.
Add posts on the edges of each fence with the liner brush and Bittersweet Chocolate. Highlight post with Bittersweet + White.

FINISHING

Pull a few branches in the background trees with thinned Bittersweet Chocolate using the liner brush.
Make it snow by loading an old toothbrush with thinned

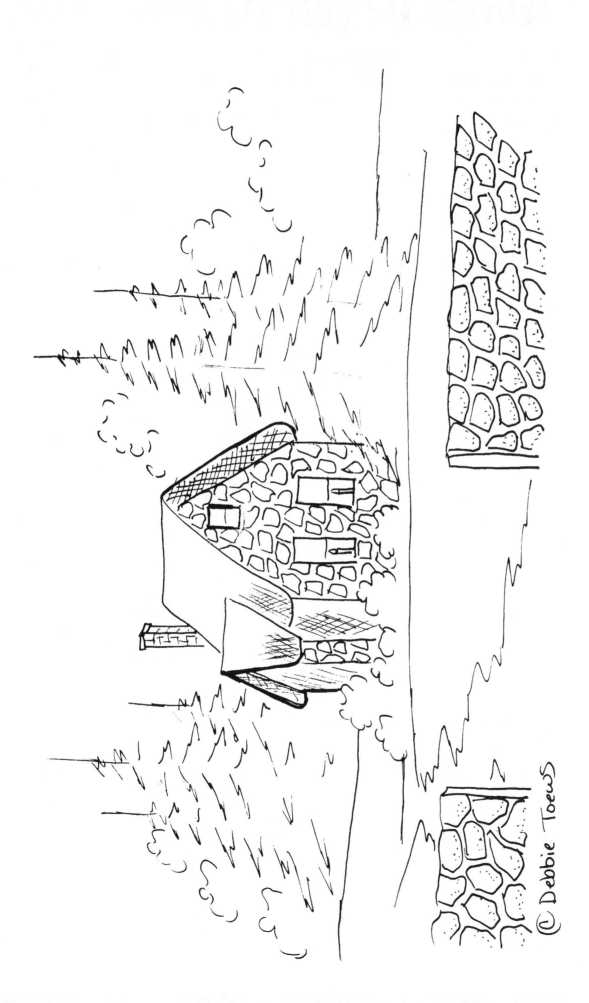

© Debbie Toews

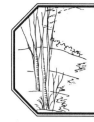

White Birch River
sap bucket
color photo on page 21 • pattern on page 25

Paint Palette

Krylon Spray Paints
#3505 Colonial Blue Satin
3501 Navy Satin

DecoArt Americana

Titanium White	Midnight Green
Country Red	Lamp Black
French Grey Blue	Raw Sienna
Buttermilk	Midnight Blue
Bittersweet Chocolate	

Special Supplies
Metal Sap Bucket
DecoArt Spray Sealer/Finisher

Preparation
Wash metal with a vinegar/water solution to remove any oily residue.
Spray entire outside of bucket with Navy Blue Satin, let dry thoroughly.

Painting Instructions

SKY
Spray in sky with Colonial Blue Satin using a tight circular motion, staying about 6- 8 inches away from surface of bucket. You want this to be contained in a large circle, approximately 3 or 4 inches from the top of the bucket.

PINE TREES
Paint in the lighter colored pines first. Start the tree with an 18/0 liner brush forming the very top and first few boughs using a mix of French Grey Blue + touch of Midnight Green + touch of White. Pick up an old worn shader and stipple in rest of tree working from the middle, out, on each bough. It will only be necessary to work part way down as they will be covered toward the bottom by the other trees.
Pines in the foreground are basically painted in the same manner. Use the liner and Midnight Green to paint a straight line down the middle of each pine for placement. Leave at least a ½ inch at top before brushing in the first few small boughs with the liner brush. Stipple in rest of tree with the old shader. It will go a bit faster if you want to basecoat across the bottom half (of the trees) with a large brush and Midnight Green. Then just simply stipple over it for texture, this way you won't have to worry about the thickness of the trees, the depth will already be there! Wash out brush, when trees are dry, stipple on a bit of White for snow.

BRIDGE
Base in left side of bridge with the #10 and Country Red + touch of Buttermilk. Right side is Country Red + touch of Black. Wash out brush, streak left side lightly with Buttermilk

for added texture. With the #4 paint in windows, underneath eave and opening with Lamp Black.
Use a #10 to brush in roof with Titanium White. Pull from the bottom of the roof, up, with French Grey Blue, blending into the White (for shading).
Frame roof with a thin line of White using the 18/0 liner brush. Frame windows and door with thinned Raw Sienna + Buttermilk. Outline to the right and bottom of framing with a thin line of Black for more definition.
Use the #4 and a thin wash of Lamp Black to cast a shadow under the roof.
Pull down a few icicles and add snow to the windows with the liner brush and thinned White.

WATER
With the #10 base in water (working from left to right) with French Grey Blue + touch of White. Darken edges of water by pulling from outer edge, to the inside, with Midnight Blue + touch of Black. Moisten your brush a bit if you are having trouble getting it to blend into the base color (French Grey Blue). Wash out brush, streak White (horizontally) up the middle for a "rippled" effect.

SNOW
Lay in snow with the #12 and thinned Titanium White. (It will help the paint to stick a bit easier if you basecoat it a couple of times first)!

As you work down, pick up French Grey Blue for shading at the bottom of each slope, blending this up into the White. Highlight each slope by adding more White, blending down into the Blue. When laying the snow into the water turn your brush on the tip and gently slope into the water. After snow is dry, pick up a little of Bittersweet Chocolate + Raw Sienna and scrub along the shore line for a "muddy" look!

BIRCH TREES
Paint in birch trees using the #2 for the largest part of the trunk and the 0 liner for the thinner branches. Base in with White + Buttermilk. Pull around left side of tree with Raw Sienna, using a very light amount of paint. This should look "streaky", like bark. With the 18/0 liner and thinned Bittersweet Chocolate, pull a few blades of dead grass around the bottom of the tree trunks. Lay snow in underneath to "set them in".

FINISHING
Make it snow by loading an old toothbrush with thinned White, aiming the brush at the surface and pulling back gently on the bristles.

Spray with DecoArt Sealer/Finisher. Or if you prefer a more durable finish (for outside), brush on DecoArt Duraclear Varnish.

"White Birch River"
pattern
directions on page 20

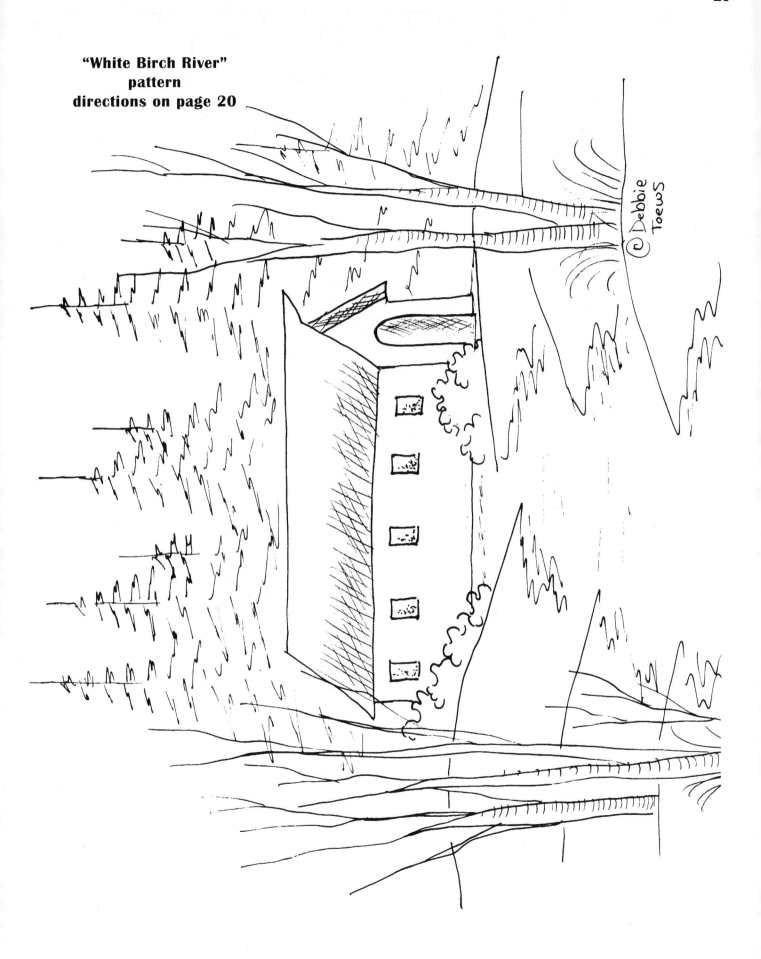

The Chicken Coop
blue canning jar
color photo on page 21 • pattern on this page

Paint Palette

Krylon Spray Paint
#3505 Colonial Blue Satin
#3501 Navy Satin

DecoArt Americana
Titanium White
Khaki Tan
Bittersweet Chocolate
Raw Sienna
French Grey Blue
Country Red
Lamp Black
Buttermilk
Slate Grey

Special Supplies
Blue Canning Jar
(1qt.)
2" foam pillow form
(for sponging trees)
DecoArt Spray Sealer
Finisher/or Enviro-Tex
(if you want a more
permanent finish)

Grey, so it looks like an easy graduation of color from light to dark. Rings around silo are Black, painted with the 18/0 liner, highlight on the left side of rings with White. Outline top of silo with White

Paint in left side of coop with the #10 and Country Red. Streak lightly with

Preparation
No special preparation needed. Wash your jar in warm soapy water to remove any residue, other than that, the spray paint will be your painting base.

Painting Instructions

SKY
Spray sky in with Navy Satin. Use a small circular motion, spraying 6-8 inches from surface. Next spray in Colonial Blue toward the upper middle of the Navy, leaving at least 2 inches of Navy showing at the top.

TREES
Sponge in trees using a small piece of the pillow form rolled to form a loose ball. Dip sponge in Khaki Tan tipped in White. Pat in trees starting at horizon and working up, varying the size and shapes of the trees. Tip sponge in extra White, patting on more "White" for added snow.
*Basecoat ground area with White.

CHICKEN COOP & SILO
Silo is brushed in with the #10 and Slate Grey. Shade right side with Black, blending this over into the Grey. Highlight left side with White, again, blending this over into the Slate

Buttermilk for added texture, forming more of a "board" look. Base in right side with Country Red + touch of Black. Paint in windows with the #4 and Lamp Black.

Use the 0 liner to paint underneath eave Black. With the smaller liner (18/0), frame roof and windows, and paint in crossbars (in windows) with thinned Raw Sienna + Buttermilk. Outline bottom and right side of window frames with a thin line of Black for added definition. Outline top of roof with White for "snow"!

Cast a shadow under roof with the #6 and a thin wash of Black.

SNOW
Lay in snow using the #12 and Titanium White. As you work down and to the right of the coop lay in shading with French Blue Grey. The two colors should blend together so you see a graduation of color from light to dark. If the brush gets too dry and starts to drag, add a touch of water to make the blending easier.

FENCE
Paint in fence posts using the 0 liner and Bittersweet Chocolate starting on the right side. Keep strokes short and choppy so they look like old wood! Highlight to the left of the post with

(continued on page 27)

Raw Sienna, and then with Buttermilk, slightly blending the colors together just a bit.

Wire around the fence is brushed in with thinned Black using the 18/0 liner.

Also with the smaller liner, bring up a few blades of dead grass and branches with thinned Bittersweet Chocolate. Lay White on some of these for "snow". Add small dots on the branches in Country Red for berries.

Lay some White in under fence posts to set them in.

FINISHING

Add a few branches to the trees with thinned Bittersweet Chocolate.

Make it snow by loading an old toothbrush with thinned White, aiming at the surface and pulling back on the bristles.

Spray jar with DecoArt Finisher/Sealer or use Enviro-Tex coating if you want a glossier more permanent finish.

Bumblebees & Birdhouses
large crockery birdhouse
color photo on page 22 • pattern on page 28

Paint Palette

Krylon Spray Paints
#3505 Colonial Blue Satin
#1509 Navajo White

DecoArt Americana

Yellow Light	Hauser Dark Green
Bittersweet Chocolate	Titanium White
Lamp Black	Buttermilk
Raw Sienna	Peony Pink
Country Blue	French Grey Blue
Brilliant Red	True Blue

Special Supplies

Large Crockery Birdhouse
DecoArt Duraclear Interior/Exterior Varnish

Preparation

Wash crockery with warm soapy water to remove any residue, dry thoroughly.

Painting Instructions

SKY

Spray in sky with Colonial Blue Satin. When dry, spray in Navajo White, toward the middle of the blue, extending this more than half way down the crock.

ROCK FENCE

With the #12 shader, base in fence with Lamp Black. Use the #8 to form stones, loading with Raw Sienna tipped in Buttermilk on the top and French Grey Blue on the bottom of the brush. Lay stones in loosely, varying the size and shapes. Keep the Buttermilk to the top of the stone for highlight. You may be able to work a couple of stones before picking up color again, but as you work you will loose the highlight so you may want to go back after you have painted all of them and lay in some more Buttermilk toward the top of each stone.

BIRDHOUSES

Blue birdhouse is painted in with the #10 using French Grey Blue. Streak lightly with White for texture. Use the liner brush to paint in underneath eave and bird holes with Black. Frame roof and left side of bird holes with White. Outline top left of roof frame with a thin line of Black. Use the #4 to cast a shadow under the roof line with a thin wash of Black.

The middle birdhouse is based in with Buttermilk, streaking lightly with Raw Sienna. The underneath eave and bird hole is Black, framing the roof and bird hole with Raw Sienna + Buttermilk. Paint the perch in with Raw Sienna. Also cast a shadow under left side of roof with a thin wash of Black.

Platform and post for this birdhouse and the next are both painted with the 0 liner starting on the left with Bittersweet Chocolate. Make your brush strokes "choppy" as you work down with your color so it looks like old wood. Highlight to the right of post and top of platform with Raw Sienna + Buttermilk.

The "log" birdhouse is based in with the #6 and Raw Sienna, streaking (horizontally) with Buttermilk. Separate logs by floating Bittersweet Chocolate across the bottom of each one. Underneath eave and bird hole is Black, Roof is Buttermilk with a touch of Raw Sienna. Again, cast a shadow under the roof on the left side.

FLOWERS

Stipple in foliage using an old worn brush and Dark Hauser Green + touch of Bittersweet Chocolate. Highlight foliage with Dark Hauser tipped in Yellow Light.

Wash out brush, stipple on flowers in varying shades of Country Blue tipped in White, Peony tipped in White and Brilliant Red tipped in White. The topiary is stippled on with the dark green mix and highlighted on the left with Yellow Light.

The trunk is a line of Bittersweet Chocolate, highlighting with Raw Sienna + Buttermilk.

FINISHING

Bumblebees are painted in with the 18/0 liner and Yellow Light. Stripe and detail bees and paint dashes with Lamp Black. Wings are washes of White (painted with the #1 shader), outlined in Black.

Finish with DecoArt Duraclear Interior/Exterior Varnish for outdoor durability.

"Bumblebees & Birdhouse"
pattern

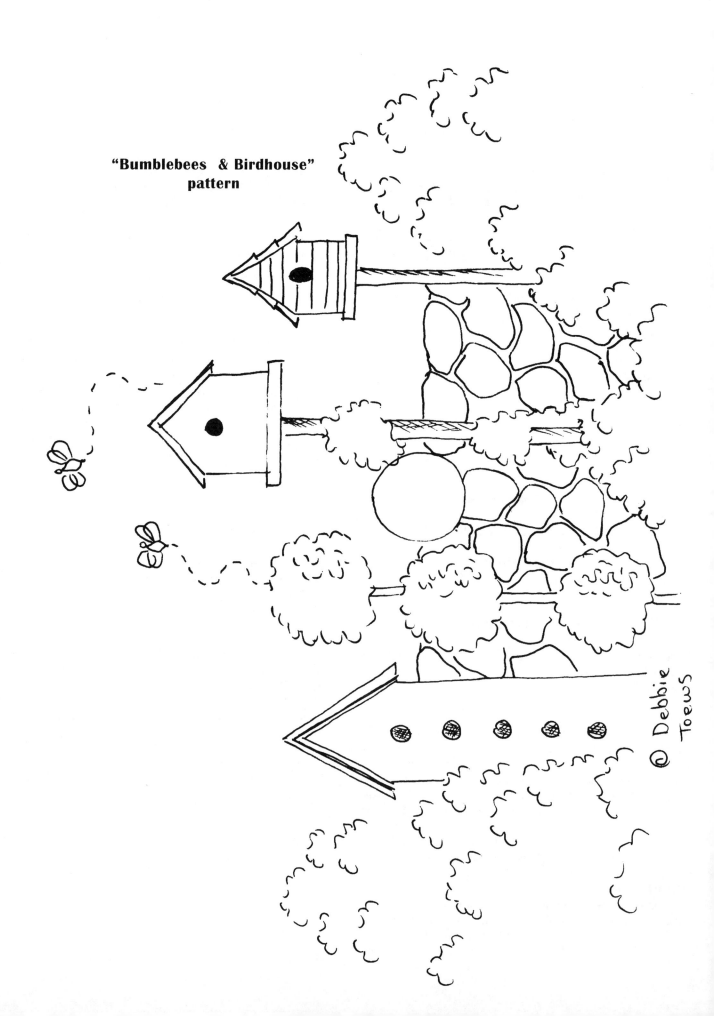

© Debbie Toews

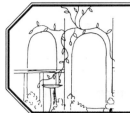

Springtime Gazebo
gazebo bird feeder
color photo on page 22 • pattern on this page

Paint Palette

DecoArt Americana

Petal Pink
Neutral Grey
Lamp Black
French Grey Blue
Midnight Green
Royal Fuchsia
Brilliant Red
Marigold
Yellow Light
Limeade

Titanium White
Heritage Brick
Buttermilk
Raw Sienna
Jade Green
Country Blue

Special Supplies

Wood Gazebo
2" foam pillow form for
sponging on color
Deco Art Duraclear
Interior/Exterior Varnish
DecoArt Wood Sealer

Preparation

Lightly sand any rough edges. Seal with DecoArt wood sealer.

Painting Instructions

GAZEBO

Use a large brush to basecoat gazebo with Petal Pink. Tear off a large piece of sponge, roll to form a loose ball, dip into White and sponge outside of gazebo with White, blending a bit, creating a "mottled" look.

Tear off another piece of sponge, base roof White by patting on a heavy amount of color. Using a smaller piece of sponge, pat on Neutral Grey down each corner (or bend) of the roof, pouncing until the shade is blended softly into the White.

With a #12 shader paint bottom platform with Titanium White.

FENCE

Paint in fence using the #2 shader and 0 liner. Base in posts with Titanium White.
Shade to the right and bottom with a thin line of Neutral Grey using the 0 liner.

© Debbie Toews

BIRDBATH

Brush in bird bath with the #2 and Neutral Grey. Highlight the pedestal with White, blending this over into the Grey.

CLAY POT

Paint in pot using the #6 and Heritage Brick. Highlight on the left with Buttermilk, blending this over into the Brick. Wash out brush, pick up Black for shading and pull this down on the right side, blending over into the Heritage Brick.

BIRDHOUSE

Base in the birdhouse with the #6 and French Grey Blue + White on the left and French Grey Blue + touch of Black on the right. Wash out brush, streak down lightly on left side with White for added texture.
Roof is Raw Sienna, highlighting by pulling down from top edge with Buttermilk.
Use to 0 liner to paint in underneath eave and bird holes with Black.
With the 18/0 liner frame roof with thinned Buttermilk + touch of Raw Sienna. Frame right side of bird holes with Buttermilk. Underline roof framing on right with a thin line of Black for more definition.

BEEHIVE

Beehive is painted with the #4 and Marigold. Do not wash gold out of brush, pick up Raw Sienna on the bottom tip and pull across under each layer with shading.
Wash out brush, pick up a bit of Yellow Light on the tip of brush and pull across top of each layer with this highlight.
Use the liner to paint the hole in the front, outline to the right of hole with thinned Buttermilk using the 18/0 liner.

FOLIAGE & FLOWERS

Use an old worn brush to stipple on foliage with Midnight Green. Highlight foliage by stippling on a bit of Jade Green.
Wash out brush, stipple on flowers in alternate shades of Country Blue tipped in White, Royal Fuchsia tipped in White, Brilliant Red tipped in White.

VINE

Paint in branches with the 18/0 and thinned Bittersweet Chocolate. Highlight branches with Raw Sienna + Buttermilk. Leaves are based in with Midnight Green, highlighting by pulling around the top with Limeade.

FINISHING

Finish by brushing on a coat of DecoArt Duraclear Indoor/Outdoor Varnish.

"Summertime Blues" thermometer pattern

"Summertime Blues" clay pot pattern

© Debbie Toews

Summertime Blues
clay pot, stepping stone, thermometer, edging
color photos on pages 22 & 23 • pattern on pages 30, 32-34

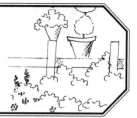

Paint Palette

DecoArt Patio Paints

Hydrangea Blue	Blue Bell
Concrete Grey	Cloud Grey
Wrought Iron Black	Petunia Purple
Woodland Brown	Golden Honey
Patio Brick	Pine Green
Sunshine Yellow	Sprout Green
Red Pepper	Buttercup Yellow
Summer Sky Blue	Fuchsia
Daisy Cream	Clear Coat

Special Supplies

Concrete Flower Bed Edging, stepping stone, clay pot (any home & garden center)
Wood Thermometer
2" foam pillow form (for sponging background color)
DecoArt Wood Sealer
Rubbing Alcohol

Preparation

Sand any rough edges of thermometer. Apply wood sealer to front and back.
Wipe off all concrete and clay pieces with rubbing alcohol to remove any concrete/clay residue, let dry thoroughly before painting.

PAINTING INSTRUCTIONS

(Thin paints using the clear coat)

BACKGROUNDS

Sponge in blue background using a large piece of the pillow form (rolled up) starting at the top with Hydrangea, working about 1/4 of the way down. Pick up
a new piece of sponge and pat in Blue Bell as you work down, patting gently where the two colors meet to blend them together. When you get half way down pick up Blue Bell + White (clean sponge) and pat down to the bottom to cover the surface.
Sponge or basecoat with a large brush the back and sides with Hydrangea.

FENCE

Fence posts are painted in with the #10 and Cloud White. Use the 0 liner or #2 to paint in shaded side of post with Concrete Grey. Lattice on thermometer is brushed in with White using the liner.

FLOWERS

(Some flowers must have the clay pots painted first).
Stipple in foliage for flowers (either with a small piece of sponge or a large worn flat brush) using Pine Green + touch of Woodland Brown. Stipple on highlight for foliage with Sprout Green + Sunshine Yellow.
Wash out brush and use alternate colors to stipple on flowers. Shades will range from Lavender tipped in White, Fuchsia tipped in White, Red tipped in White and Summer Sky (delphiniums) with Summer Sky + White for petals. Make petals on delphinium with the 0 liner. The edging has a few white daisies on it that are small dots of White (made with the end of the brush), with Sunshine Yellow centers.

CLAY POTS

Using the #8, paint in clay pot with Patio Brick. Highlight on left side with Patio Brick + Daisy Cream, blending over into the base color. Shade on right side with Brick + touch of Black, again, blending over into the middle. Highlight the lip of the pot with Daisy Cream.

BEEHIVES

Paint in beehives with Sunshine Yellow + touch of Golden Honey. Shade by tipping edge of brush in Golden Honey and pulling around the bottom of each layer with the shading. Highlight outer edges and top of each layer with Sunshine Yellow + touch of White. Beehive hole is put in with the liner and Black. Outline right edge of hole with a thin line of White. Wood posts are short choppy strokes of Woodland Brown on the right (with the 0 liner), highlighting with Honey Brown + Daisy Cream on the left.

WOOD BUTTERFLY & BIRDHOUSE

(on stepping stone and edging)
Using the #6 paint in left side of house with Honey Brown + touch of Daisy Cream, (mix your paint loosely so you see a variation of color). Base in right side of house with Honey Brown + Woodland Brown. Roof is Concrete Grey, pulling down from the top with a touch of White for added highlight. Pull in a bit of Patio Brick over the roof for a "rusty" look. Paint in underneath eave and holes with the liner brush and Black. Frame roof with a thin line of White, underlining with a thin line of Black for added definition.

PINK BIRDHOUSES

The pink birdhouses are brushed in with Carnation Pink on the left (#6), streaking lightly with White for added texture. Right side is brushed in with Carnation + touch of Black. Roof is White, pulling up from the bottom with Concrete Grey for shading. Underneath eave and Bird holes are Black brushed in with the 18/0 liner. Frame roof with thinned White

TALL BIRDHOUSE

Birdhouse is based in with Buttercup Yellow on the left, streaking lightly with White. Right side is Buttercup + touch of Golden Honey. Roof is Golden Honey, highlighting by pulling down from top with Daisy Cream. Underneath eave and bird holes are painted in with the liner brush and Black. Perches and platform are Golden Honey.

Frame roof with the liner and thinned Daisy Cream

TOPIARIES

Stipple in topiaries with an old worn brush using Pine Green + touch of Woodland Brown. Highlight on the left side with Sprout Green + touch of Sunshine Yellow.

Stems are Woodland Brown, highlighted with Golden Honey + Daisy Cream painted with the 18/0 liner. Topiary (on the thermometer), have small dots of Red Pepper for the berries.

"Summertime Blues" pattern for edging

"Summertime Blues" pattern for edging

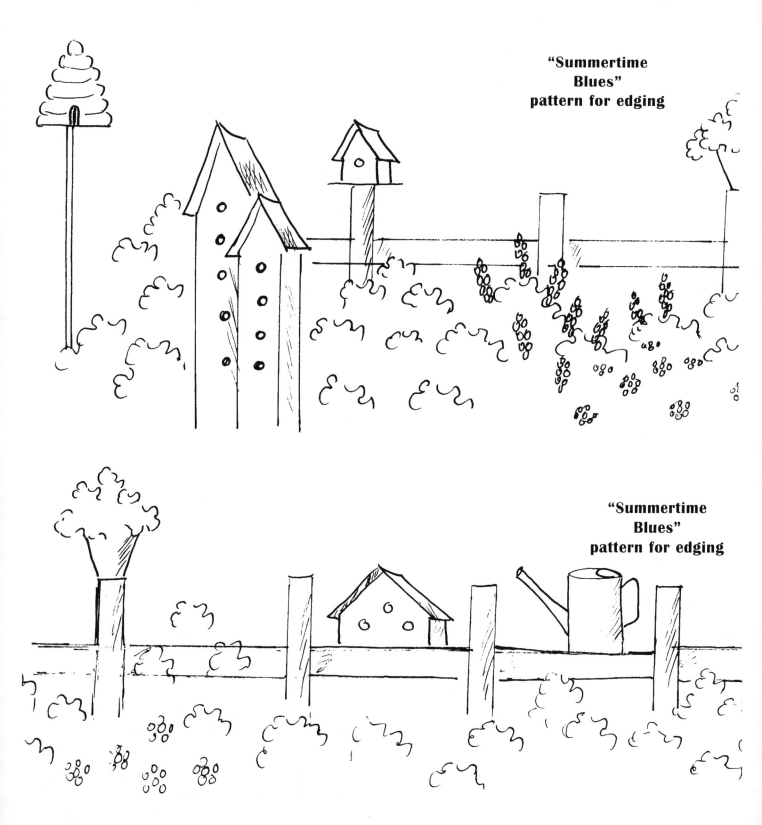

WATERING CAN

Using the #4 base in can with Concrete Grey. Shade on the right side and bottom of spout with a touch of Black, blending into the Grey. Highlight on the left with White, also blending into the Grey. With the liner paint inside of can with Concrete Grey + touch of Black. Outline top rim of can with a thin line of White.

BEES & BUTTERFLY

Bees are painted in with the liner and Sunshine Yellow. Paint stripes and small details with Black. Wings are brushed in using a wash of White, outlining with a thin line of White.
Butterfly is brushed in using Sunshine Yellow + touch of Red Pepper (to make orange). Paint lines and details in with thinned Black.
Paint in dashes with small lines of Black.

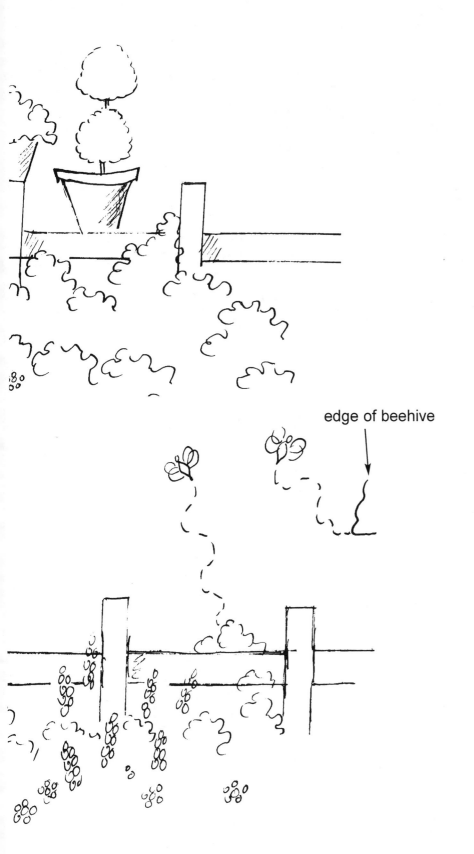

edge of beehive

"Summertime
Blues"
stepping stone
pattern

Silent Snow
Round tin
color photo on page 24 • pattern on following page

Paint Palette

Krylon Spray Paints
#3505 Colonial Blue Satin
#3501 Navy Blue Satin

DecoArt Americana

French Blue Grey	Khaki Tan
Titanium White	Country Red
Raw Sienna	Lamp Black
Slate Grey	Bittersweet Chocolate
Buttermilk	

Special Supplies

Primed Metal Tin
2" foam pillow form (for sponging in trees)
DecoArt Spray Matte Finisher/Sealer

Preparation

No preparation necessary other than spraying entire tin with Navy Blue Satin.

Painting Instructions

SKY
Spray in sky with Colonial Blue Satin leaving at least 2 or 3 inches of Navy showing at the top. Extend the Colonial Blue about half way down the tin.

TREES
Pat in trees, using a piece of sponge rolled to form a loose ball, with Khaki Tan tipped in White. Start at the bottom (horizon) and work up, varying the size and shapes. "Highlight" trees with more White (toward the top) for extra "snow".

BARNS & SILOS
Silos are painted in using a # 10 shader and Slate Grey. Shade to the right side with Black, blending this over into the Grey. (Pick up a bit of water on the brush if it starts to drag). Wash out brush, and highlight on the left with White, again, blending this over into the base color (Grey).
With the 18/0 liner paint in rings around silo, and outline top with thinned White.

Barns are based in with the same brush using Country Red + touch of Buttermilk on the left and Country Red + touch of Black on the right. Wash out brush and streak lightly over left side with a bit more Buttermilk for added texture. Streak lightly over right side with Country Red.
Barn door is painted in using the dark mix, (Red + Black).
Underneath eaves, door on small barn and windows are all brushed in using the #2 and Lamp Black.
Roof is brushed in using the #10 and Slate Grey. Wash out brush, bring snow down on roof using Titanium White, starting at the top and pulling down, following the contour of the roof. Frame windows and doors with the liner brush and thinned Raw Sienna + touch of Buttermilk. Frame roof with thinned White. Outline to the left and underneath framing with a thin line of Black for added definition.
With the #6 and a very thin wash of Lamp Black, cast a shadow under roof and to the right side of the large door by pulling down lightly with the wash of color.
Icicles can be formed by pulling down with thinned White using the 18/0 liner , varying the size of the icicles.

SNOW
Lay in snow using the #12 and thinned White. As you work down, pick up French Blue Grey and blend down. Wash out brush, pick up extra White, laying this in on the tops of the slopes and blending down. When your fence posts are completed you will go back and add more White under them to "set the in".

FENCE
Posts are painted in using either the #2 or the 0 liner, whichever you are most comfortable with! Chop in Bittersweet Chocolate down the right side of post for shading. Next, lay in Raw Sienna on the left, again using short, choppy strokes so this looks like old wood! Next to the left of the Sienna, chop in Buttermilk for highlight.
Wire is painted in with the 18/0 liner and thinned Black. Outline some of the wire and top of fence posts with a bit of White for "snow"!
Pull a few blades of dead grass and branches up around fence posts with thinned Bittersweet Chocolate, also, laying some "snow" on these.

BUCKET
Paint in bucket using a #4 and Raw Sienna. Shade right side with Bittersweet Chocolate, blending this around into the Sienna. Highlight left side with Buttermilk, also blending this into the Sienna. With the liner brush paint inside of bucket, Lamp Black. Rings around bucket and handle are Black also. Add some snow inside the bucket with the Titanium White. Set bucket in snow by brushing some White along the bottom, up over the bucket. Pull in a few blades if grass with thinned Bittersweet Chocolate.

FINISHING
Pull a few branches in the trees with the liner and thinned Bittersweet Chocolate.

Make it snow by loading an old toothbrush with thinned White. Aim brush at the surface, (handle towards you), and pull back gently on the bristles.

Finish with DecoArt spray sealer/finisher.

"Silent Snow"
pattern

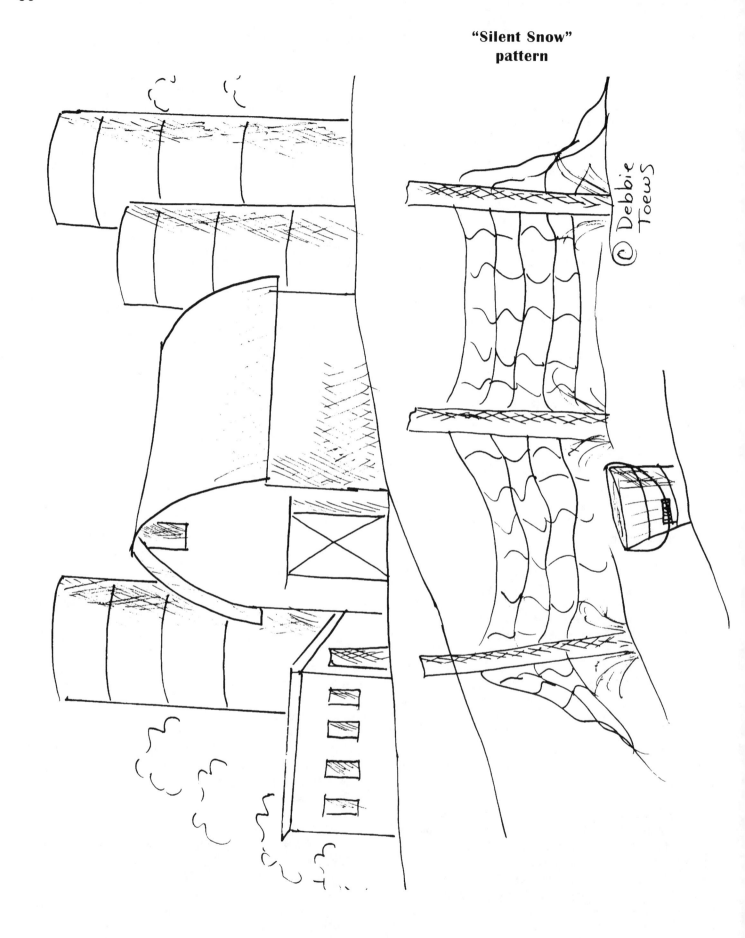

© Debbie Toews

Autumn Foliage
lantern
color photo on inside back cover • pattern on this page

Paint Palette

Krylon Spray Paint
#3505 Colonial Blue Satin
#1509 Navajo White

DecoArt Americana

Bittersweet Chocolate	Raw Sienna
Yellow Light	Primary Yellow
Brilliant Red	Cranberry
Titanium White	Uniform Blue
Lamp Black	True Ochre
Hauser Dark Green	

Special Supplies

Old Lantern
2"foam pillow form (for sponging trees)
DecoArt Spray Sealer/Finisher

Preparation

Remove globe from lantern and wash in warm soapy water, rinsing thoroughly.

Painting Instructions

SKY

Spray in sky using a tight circular motion starting with Colonial Blue first. It will be better to spray two lights coats rather than one heavy one. When dry spray on Navajo White toward the middle of the blue, leaving at least an inch or two of blue showing at the top.

TREES

Sponge in trees with a small piece of sponge, rolled to form a loose ball. Pick up a large amount of Bittersweet Chocolate, patting from horizon, up, varying the size and shapes of the trees. Use a new piece of sponge for highlights. Double or triple load sponge with Cranberry/Brilliant Red/Yellow Light , Raw Sienna/ Primary Yellow, and Brilliant Red/ Yellow Light. Dip into color and tip sponge in the lighter (highlight) shade. Keep the highlight to the top and pat in "arches" of color starting at the tops of the trees and working down, leaving some darkness showing in between for "depth".

PINE TREE

Form a straight line for top of pine with the 18/0 liner and Hauser Dark Green + touch of Black. Leave about and ½ of an inch before forming a few small boughs from each side of the middle line. Pick up an old worn brush (a #6 flat works well) and stipple in the rest of the pine working from the middle, out, on each bough.
Use the chiseled edge of the brush for more control!
Highlight on tops of boughs with Yellow Light.
•Base in grass area with True Ochre

HOUSE

Using a #8 base in left side of house with Buttermilk. Right side is Buttermilk + touch of Black. Streak left side lightly with a touch of the dark mix for added texture.
Windows and underneath eave are brushed in with the #4 and Black.
Roof and shutters are based in with Uniform Blue. Shade bottom of roof by pulling up with Uniform Blue + touch of Black. Highlight top of roof with a touch of Buttermilk, blending into the blue. Use the 18/0 liner to paint lines on shutters and crossbars in windows with thinned White.
Trim on house is Uniform Blue, framing around roof is Uniform Blue + White. Underline all framing on right and bottom with a thin line of Black for added definition. Cast a shadow under left side of roof with the #4 and a thin wash of Black.

SHRUBBERY

Stipple in shrubbery with the old brush (same as used for the pine) and Hauser Dark Green + touch of Black. Highlight with Yellow Light.

© Debbie Toews

GRASS

Using the #2 mini fan, pat in grass starting at the horizon and working down with True Ochre. As you work down pick up

(continued on page 38)

(continued from page 37)

Brilliant Red + Raw Sienna for shading, patting until one color blends nicely into the other. Wash out brush, highlight tops of slopes with Yellow Light + touch of White, blending this down into the base color. Refer to picture for shading placement.

FENCE

The fence posts are simply lines formed with the liner brush and Titanium White.

Shade on the right side of each post with a grey shade (White + touch of Black).
Pat in grass along fence line to "set" posts in.

FINISHING

Birds are painted with the 18/0 liner and thinned Black.
Pull a few branches inside of trees with thinned Raw Sienna + touch of Buttermilk with the liner brush.
Finish with DecoArt Spray Sealer/Finisher.

Golden Harvest
oval metal planter
color photo on inside back cover • pattern on next page

Paint Palette

Krylon Spray Paints
#3505 Colonial Blue Satin   #1509 Navajo White

DecoArt Americana Metal Paints
Bright White   Antique Lace
Burnt Sienna

DecoArt Americana Acrylics:
Bittersweet chocolate   Raw Sienna
Primary Yellow   Brilliant Red
Yellow Light   Hauser Dark Green
Cranberry   Country Red
True Ochre   Buttermilk
Lamp Black   Titanium White
Slate Grey

Special Supplies
Metal planter
2" foam pillow form for sponging trees
Deco Art Spray Sealer/ Finisher
Masking tape

Preparation
Wash metal with a vinegar/water solution to remove any oily residue.

Painting Instructions
Tape off the rusty tin bands to protect them from unwanted paint. Using a large piece of sponge, pat on basecoat with metal paints, using Antique Lace dipped in White for a "mottled" look. When dry, spatter with Burnt Sienna.

SKY
Spray in sky using Colonial Blue first. Spray in a circular motion keeping can at least 6 to 8 inches away from surface. It will be best to spray two light coats rather than one heavy one! When blue is dry spray in Navajo White toward the middle of the blue.

TREES
Sponge in trees using a 2" piece of foam torn off from the pillow form. Roll to form a loose ball, dip in Bittersweet Chocolate and pat in the "depth" of the trees starting and the horizon, working up. Highlight, (using a new piece of sponge for each color), with alternate colors of Hauser Dark Green tipped in Yellow Light, Brilliant red tipped in Yellow Light and Raw Sienna tipped in Primary Yellow.
When highlighting, start at the tops of the trees and work down, being careful not to cover too much of the dark or you'll lose your "depth".

*Base in ground area with True Ochre.

BARNS AND SILOS
Use a #8 to base in silos with Slate Grey. Shade right side with Black, blending this over into the base color (Grey). Highlight left sides with White, again, walking this around and blending it over into the Grey. You want to see a graduation of color from light to dark. Use the 18/0 liner to paint in rings and outline top with thinned Black. Outline top with a thin line of White.

Base in left side of barns with the #8 and Country Red. Right (or shaded) sides are Country Red + touch of Black. Streak the left side lightly with Buttermilk so it looks like "old wood". Streak the right sides lightly with Country Red. Paint in the door on the large barn with the dark mix using a #6.
Roofs will be painted in with the #8 using Raw Sienna + Slate Grey. Shade at the bottom by pulling up with Bittersweet Chocolate blending into the Sienna. Highlight by pulling down with a touch of Buttermilk.

Brush in windows and underneath eave with the #2 or #4 and Lamp Black.

Frame roof, windows, and door with thinned Raw Sienna + Buttermilk using the 18/0 liner.

(I added a touch more Buttermilk to this mix for the "front" or left sides of the barns).

Underline framing under the roof with a thin line of Black for added definition.

"Cast a shadow" under the roof using the #6 and a very thin wash of Black.

WINDMILL

Paint in tower of windmill using the liner brush and inky Black.

Highlight on the left side with Slate Grey.

Blades are painted in with either the #2 or the liner (whichever you are more comfortable using) and Black + touch of White. Inside, or details on blades are brushed in with Black. Outline a few of the blades on the top and left side with a thin lines of White for highlight.

GRASS

Pat in grass with the #2 fan brush using True Ochre. As you work down, shade bottom of slopes and to the right side of the barns with Brilliant Red + Raw Sienna.

Wash out brush and highlight tops of slopes with Yellow Light + touch of White.

Pat, wipe color out of brush, and continue patting until one color blends into the other.

FINISHING

Pull a few tree branches in with the 18/0 and Raw Sienna + touch of Buttermilk.

Branches above the tree line are Bittersweet Chocolate.

Birds are Black.

Finish with DecoArt Spray Sealer/Finisher.

"Golden Harvest" pattern

©Debbie Toews

Birdhouse Votive

crockery votive holder *(shown with plant)*
color photo on back cover • pattern on this page

Paint Palette

Krylon Spray Paint

#3503 Colonial Blue Satin
#1509 Navajo White

DecoArt Americana

Titanium White	Lamp Black
Yellow Light	Brilliant Red
Bittersweet Chocolate	Raw Sienna
Buttermilk	Uniform Blue

Special Supplies

Crockery Votive Holder
DecoArt Spray Sealer/Finisher

Painting Instructions

SKY

Spray in sky with Colonial Blue using a very small circular motion. When dry, spray in Navajo White aiming toward the middle, bottom of the crock.

FLOWERS

Use an old brush to stipple in background of flowers with Bittersweet Chocolate + touch of Raw Sienna. Wash out brush, stipple on flowers in alternate shades of Brilliant Red tipped in Yellow Light and Raw Sienna tipped in Yellow Light.

FENCE

Posts are put in with the 18/0 liner using Bittersweet Chocolate. Highlight with Raw Sienna + Buttermilk.

Wire are thin lines of Black.

BIRDHOUSE

Base in birdhouse with the #4 and White on the left, White + touch of Black on the right. Roof is Uniform Blue, highlighting by pulling from the top with White.
Underneath eave and bird holes are Black painted with the 18/0 liner. Frame roof with White, underlining framing with a thin line of Black for added definition.
Perches are Uniform Blue.

FINISHING

Birds are painted in with the liner using Black. Add a few more flowers over the fence posts to "set them in".

© Debbie Toews

Falling Leaves

frame with shelf and pegs
color photo on back cover • pattern on page 42

Paint Palette

Krylon Spray Paints

#3505 Colonial Blue Satin   #3506 Rose Satin

DecoArt Americana

Raw Sienna	Light Cinnamon	Bittersweet Chocolate
Brilliant Red	True Ochre	Yellow Light
Buttermilk	True Blue	Hauser Dark Green
Titanium White	Blue Grey Mist	Primary Yellow
French Grey Blue		

Special Supplies

Framed Wood with pegs
2" foam pillow form (for sponging trees)
Autumn Leaves Stencil (Provo craft)
DecoArt Spray Sealer/Finisher

Preparation

Sand any rough edges. Basecoat insert with a mix of French Grey Blue + White.

Painting Instructions

FRAME

With a large brush, base in frame with Raw Sienna. Shade around edges by floating or sponging Light Cinnamon. (If you sponge it on, work wet on wet so it blends into the Sienna). Use small pieces of sponge to stencil on leaves in alternate shades of Hauser Dark Green, highlighting with Primary Yellow and Brilliant Red highlighting with Yellow Light. Vines are painted with the 0 liner and thinned Hauser Dark Green, highlighting these with Yellow Light.

SKY

Spray across top half of board with Colonial Blue Satin, let dry thoroughly.

Next, spray in Rose Satin, starting at middle, spraying up. Leave about 2 inches of Blue showing at the top.

BACKGROUND TREES

Sponge background trees in with a piece of pillow foam rolled to form a loose ball. Dip into Blue Grey Mist, starting at the bottom, and patting up to form the trees. Vary the shapes and sizes. Highlight, (using a different piece of sponge), with Yellow Light tipped into White. Pat off on the palette before patting onto the surface so that you have just a bit of paint on the sponge! Start at the top, working down with "arches" of color.

FOREGROUND TREES

Sponge in "depth" of trees with a new piece of sponge and Bittersweet Chocolate + Raw Sienna. Highlight with alternate shades of Raw Sienna tipped in Primary Yellow, Hauser Dark Green tipped in Yellow Light, and Brilliant Red tipped in Yellow Light. Again, vary the size and shapes of the trees, leaving the "middle" open so the Blue trees peek through the background!

MILL

Using the #10 base in mill with Raw Sienna + touch of Buttermilk. (Mix paint loosely so you see a variation of color for texture). If the boards run horizontally paint in that direction, likewise if they are running vertically.

Streak lightly with a bit of Buttermilk for added texture. Add "board" lines with the 18/0 liner and thinned Bittersweet Chocolate.

Brush in rock base, windows, and underneath eave with Lamp Black.

Using the 0 liner, frame windows and paint an "edge" down each side of the main body of the mill with thinned Buttermilk + touch of Raw Sienna.

Also with the 0 liner paint in underneath eave with Black, outlining the roof with the thinned Raw Sienna/Buttermilk mixture.

Use the 18/0 liner to paint crossbars (in window) and outline on the right and bottom of window frame with a thin line of Black.

Base inside of wheel with the #6 and Bittersweet Chocolate + touch of Black. Paint outside rim and spokes (using the #2) with Raw Sienna + Buttermilk. Outline wheel on left with a thin line of Bittersweet Chocolate to bring it out from the mill.

Outline center hub with thin line of Buttermilk. Streak spokes with a bit of Buttermilk for a weathered look!

Stones are laid in with a #4 loading the brush with a grey mix (White + touch of Black), tipping one end of the brush in Buttermilk and the other end in Raw Sienna. Lay stones in loosely, varying the shapes, but keeping the Buttermilk toward the top of the stone for "highlight".

Spout is brushed in with the grey mix. Highlight by floating White across the top. Outline opening with thin lines of White. Supports are Black, outlined with White. Cast a shadow under roof and down right side of mill with a thin wash of Black using the #6.

PINES

Start pines by painting the very top and first few boughs with the 18/0 liner and Hauser Dark Green + touch of Black. (Leave about a 1/2 inch showing at top before starting the boughs). Stipple in the rest of tree with an old worn flat brush (preferably a #6). Work from the middle, out, on each bough, making some shorter and some longer than others so its not too uniform. As you work down the tree should get larger toward the bottom and the middle should be filled in more, so you can't "see through it"! Wash out brush, highlight with a bit of Yellow Light.

WATER

Basecoat the water with the #10 using White + touch of True Blue. Work from left to right, making it wider as you work down toward the bottom of the picture. Shade each side by pulling from outer edge, in, with French Grey Blue + touch of Black. Blend this into the lighter Blue for shading.

Wash out brush, streak up the middle (working horizontally with the edge of the brush) with a touch of White. This will give it a "ripple" effect.

The shoreline is scrubbed in (around the grass area) with Bittersweet Chocolate + Raw Sienna. (Wait until after you have painted the grass before putting the shore in).

GRASS

Pat in grass with the #2 fan and True Ochre. Start at the top working from right to left and down. As you work down, pick up varying shades of Brilliant Red and/or a bit of Hauser Dark Green, patting until these are blended into the Ochre. Wash out brush, highlight toward the horizon and tops of slopes with Yellow Light + White. Lay this in (quite heavily) across the top and pat down, until blended.

Add more shading under the pines with Raw Sienna + Bittersweet Chocolate, blending down and over to the left.

FINISHING

Pull some water over the wheel with a #4 and thinned White + True Blue. Stipple on splashes (with an old brush) using White. Branches in the trees are thinned Bittersweet Chocolate painted with the 18/0 liner. Highlight left side of branches with Buttermilk + Raw Sienna.

Birds are also painted in with the liner and Black.

Spray with DecoArt Sealer/Finisher.

42

© Debbie Toews